Frog

Hug  **Bun Bun**

Little Sister

Gator

Bat Child

Maurice & Molly

Oscar

GATOR
CLEANS HOUSE

BY MERCER MAYER

RANDOM HOUSE 🏠 NEW YORK

Gator was cleaning his house. Suddenly, there was a knock on his door.

It was his friends.

"Let's go swimming," said Gator's friends.

"I can't go swimming," said Gator.

"I have to clean my house."

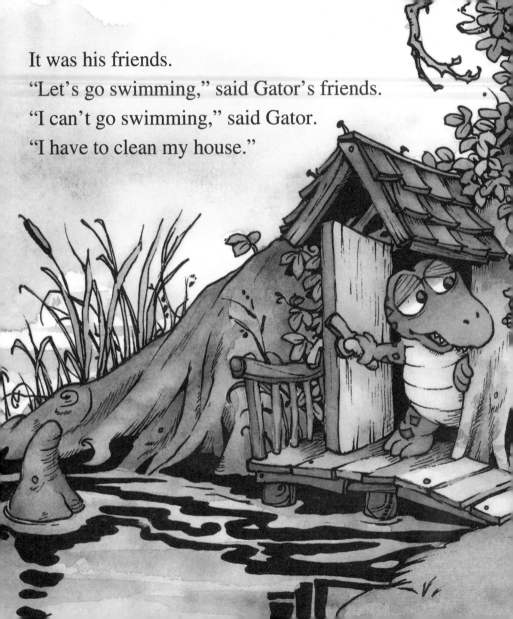

"We can help,"
said Gator's friends.
"Then you can come
swimming, too."

"I'll mop," said Little Critter.

"I'll sweep,"
said Little Sister.

"I'll dust," said Huggums.
"I'll move the chair," said Little Critter.

"Cleaning the tub is a big job," said Frog.
"Scrub-a-dub-dub."

"Time for lunch," said Little Critter.
"Good, I'm hungry," said Frog.
"Me too," said Little Sister.

After Gator's friends ate lunch,
there were a lot of dirty dishes.

"I'll wash," said Frog and Little Sister.
"I'll dry," said Max.

"Oops! Be careful with the dishes," said Little Critter.

"Gator, you take out the garbage."

"Let's make the bed," said Frog.

"Nap time," said Little Critter. "Uh-oh!
Did someone forget to turn off the water?"

After their nap, Gator's friends were ready to go. "Let's go swimming, Gator," they all said.